A special dedication of thanks
to our true heroic smile makers of our world.
Our doctors, firemen's, policemen's and women's
and a lot of other life saving technicians.

Thanks!

Their dedicated life saving service provides a lot more needed
smiles from their hearts, souls, and caring spirits.

To order additional copies of this book, contact:
Xlibris
1-888-795-4274
www.Xlibris.com
Orders@Xlibris.com

Discover the inspirational magic created from
smiles through the guidance of Mr. Sunny Sunshine.

There are never enough smiles.
Written and illustrated
by
Dwayne S. Henson

3

Why not put a smile everywhere?
Smile
Smile
Smile
Smile
Smile

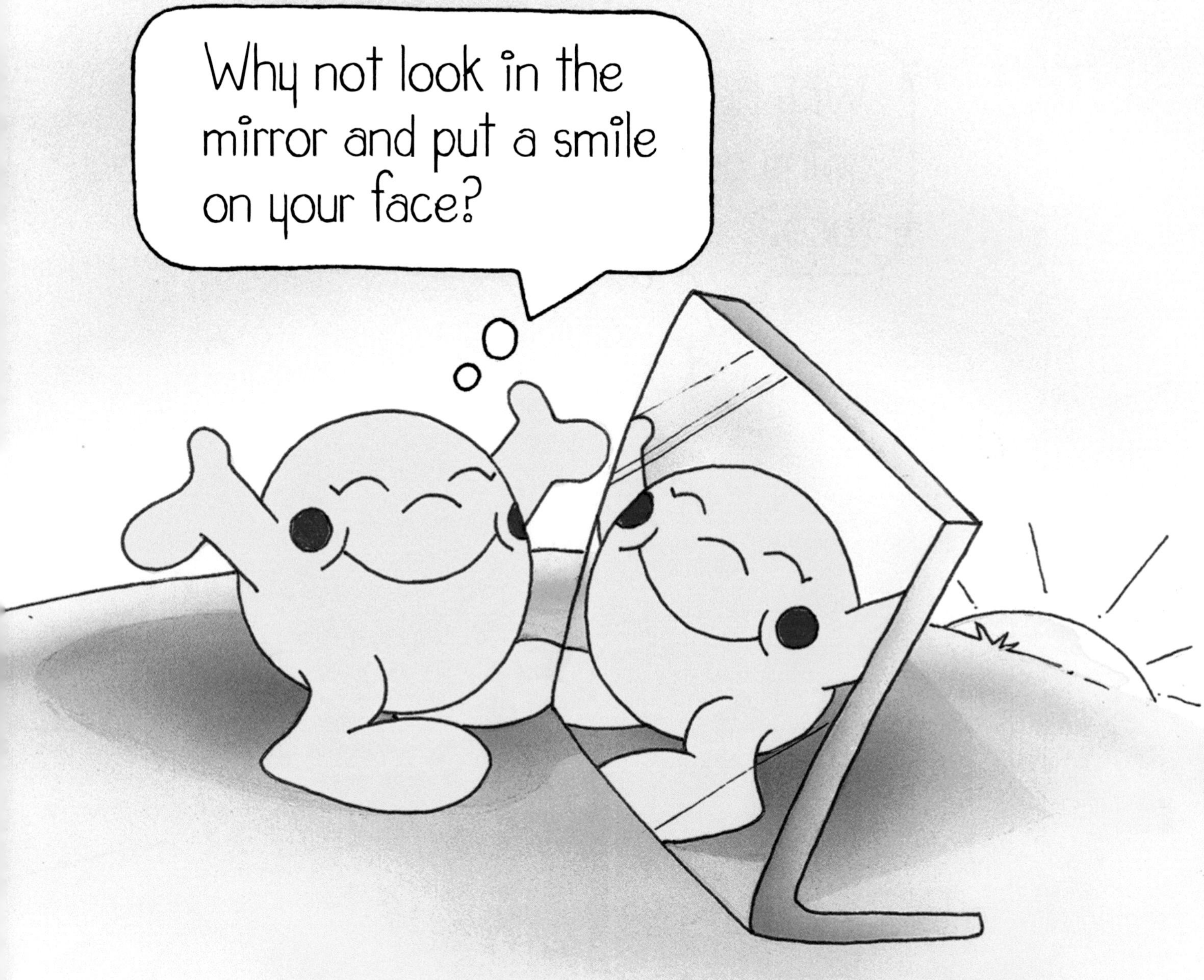
Why not look in the mirror and put a smile on your face?

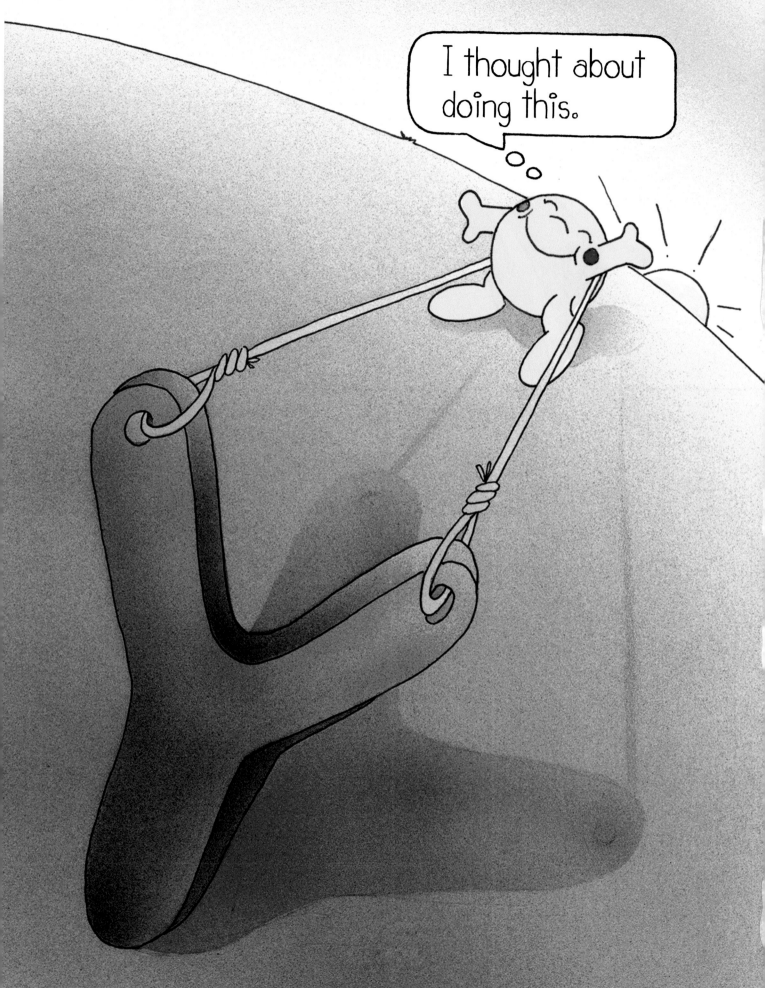

Next a special offer and a preview of more up coming Mr. Sunny Sunshine™ books. ⟶

A special offer from
the author / illustrator of the
Mr. Sunny Sunshine books
Dwayne S. Henson

← Here's my special offer.
Two preschool educational
books combined in one at
one regular sales price.

For more information on this special offer
and other Mr. Sunny Sunshine books
Contact Xlibris at: 1-888-795-4274

Dwayne S. Henson
Creator of Mr. Sunny Sunshine™

My gift that I would like to share with others is to inspire those who are in need of a smile and to educate others of the positive inspirational value that smiles provide in our society.

With Mr. Sunny Sunshine™ as my tool in this never ending educational smile-based journey. I aim to demonstrate how smiles can be utilized in so many positive encouraging ways such as to inspire, motivate, educate as well as to entertain. How Mr. Sunny Sunshine™ creates smiles and shares them with others, I truly believe, are some of the fascinating trademark dynamics of this inspiring smile making concept.

As you may come to discover there's more inspirational magic behind a smile than what we generally see.

From this unique unit of books you'll learn thow and why Mr. Sunny Sunshine™ took it upon himself to create more smiles and inspiration all over the world. Along with this you'll also be provided with a one-of-a-kind, entertaining, smile-based education and much, much, more.

There's a lot to uncover and learn about a smile. I invite you to journey along to see how truly motivating a smile can be.

I certainly hope you enjoy my Mr. Sunny Sunshine™ books as much as I did creating them for others to share. I look forward to creating lots more smiles for many of years to come.

Sincerely, Dwayne S. Henson... Prince of happiness, King of smiles.

26

Printed in the United States
By Bookmasters